THE LITTLE RED HEN

AND THE

PASSOVER MATZAH

by Leslie Kimmelman

illustrated by Paul Meisel

Holiday House / *New York*

To my friend Sharon,
a good egg
—L. K.

For Aunt Carol, Lisa,
Phil, and Kevin
—P. M.

The publisher wishes to thank Rabbi Frank Tamburello
for his expert review of this book.

Text copyright © 2010 by Leslie Kimmelman
Illustrations copyright © 2010 by Paul Meisel
All Rights Reserved
HOLIDAY HOUSE is registered in the U.S. Patent and Trademark Office.
Printed and Bound in September 2016 at Toppan Leefung, DongGuan City, China.
The text typeface is Oldavai.
The artwork was created with ink, watercolor, and pastel
on Arches watercolor paper.
www.holidayhouse.com
5 7 9 10 8 6

Library of Congress Cataloging-in-Publication Data
Kimmelman, Leslie.
The Little Red Hen and the Passover matzah / by Leslie Kimmelman;
illustrated by Paul Meisel. — 1st ed.
p. cm.
Summary: No one will help the Little Red Hen make the Passover matzah,
but they all want to help her eat it. Includes information
about Passover, a recipe for matzah,
and a glossary of Yiddish words used in the story.
ISBN 978-0-8234-1952-4 (hardcover)
ISBN 978-0-8234-2327-9 (paperback)
[1. Folklore. 2. Jews—Folklore.] I. Meisel, Paul, ill. II. Title.
PZ8.1.K568Li 2010
398.2089'924—dc22
2008048488

031721.1K4/B0969/A4

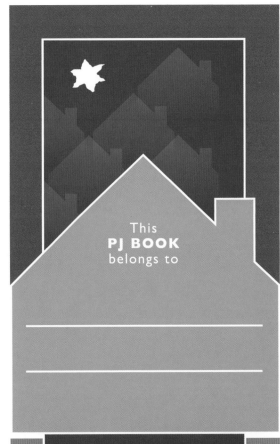

This
PJ BOOK
belongs to

PJ Library®

JEWISH BEDTIME STORIES and SONGS

The greatest wisdom of all is kindness.

—Jewish Proverb

The year was passing. The Little Red Hen could feel the change of the seasons in the tips of her tail feathers. She could smell it in the barnyard air. She could see it on her calendar. . . .

"*Oy gevalt!*" exclaimed the Little Red Hen, thinking ahead to spring. "Before I know it, it will be time for Passover. I will need some matzah for my Seder dinner, and that begins with some grains of wheat."

In a corner of the chicken coop, the Little Red Hen
kept a small pile of grains safe from wind and water.
She gathered them now and went to find her friends.
Such friends she had—always ready to lend a hand. "Who
will help me plant these grains?" she asked them.

"Not I," said Sheep.

"Sorry, bub," said Horse.

"Think again," said Dog, a little bit rudely.

The Little Red Hen was not happy. "Okay, okay," she grumbled. "I should worry? I'll just do it myself." And the Little Red Hen planted those grains.

Months passed. The sun shone, the rain fell, and the grain grew tall. The Little Red Hen waited patiently. Finally there was a field of wheat ready to be harvested. The Little Red Hen went to find her friends.

This time she was sure they'd lend a hand. "Who will help me cut the wheat?" she asked.

"Not I," said Sheep.

"Sorry, bub," said Horse.

"Think again," said Dog, a little bit rudely. "We're your friends, not your servants."

The Little Red Hen was definitely not happy. "Friends, shmends," she muttered. "I'll just do it myself." And the Little Red Hen cut the wheat.

The wheat was ready for the mill. The Little Red Hen gathered it together and went to find her friends. "They won't disappoint me again," she told herself confidently.

"Who will help me carry this wheat to the mill?" she asked them.

"Not I," said Sheep.

"Sorry, bub," said Horse.

"Think again," said Dog, a little bit rudely. "We're resting."

The Little Red Hen was *really* not happy this time. "I should live so long," she kvetched, "to see this bunch of lazy no-goodniks put in an honest day's work. I'll just do it myself."

The Little Red Hen took the wheat to a special Passover mill, where a miller ground it into flour. Then she schlepped that flour back home in a big, heavy sack, clucking to herself all the way.

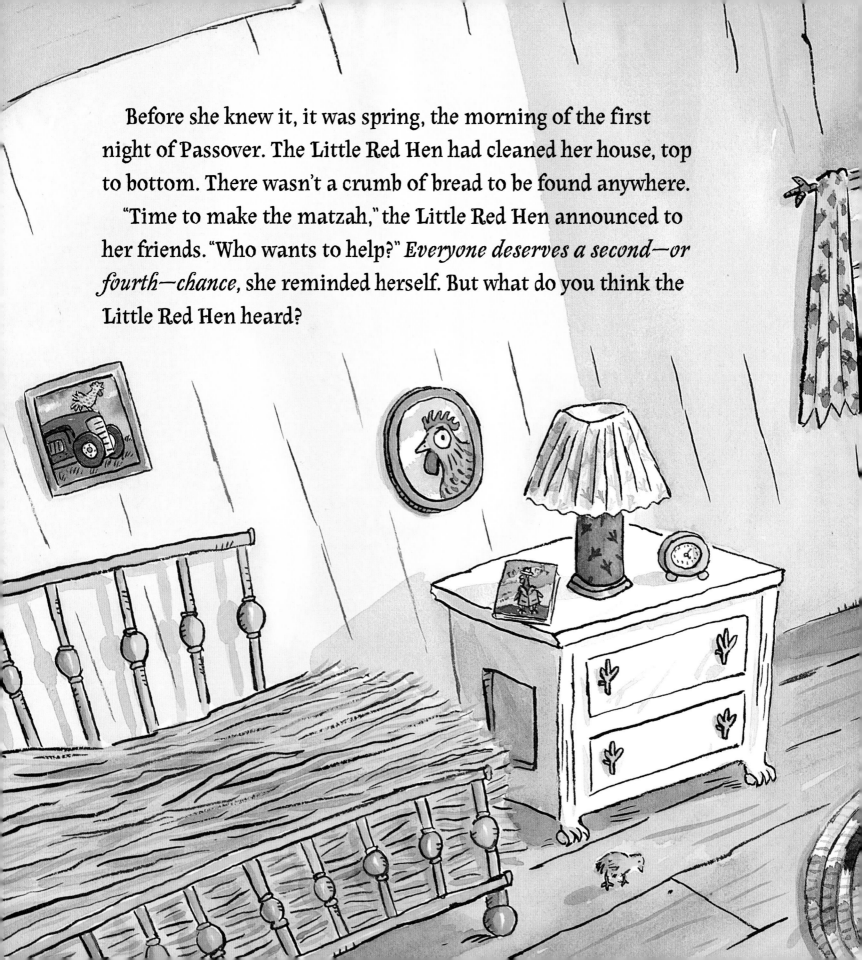

Before she knew it, it was spring, the morning of the first night of Passover. The Little Red Hen had cleaned her house, top to bottom. There wasn't a crumb of bread to be found anywhere.

"Time to make the matzah," the Little Red Hen announced to her friends. "Who wants to help?" *Everyone deserves a second—or fourth—chance*, she reminded herself. But what do you think the Little Red Hen heard?

"Not I," said Sheep.

"Sorry, bub," said Horse.

"Ha, ha," laughed Dog, more than a little bit rudely. "Think again."

The Little Red Hen was not happy. She was not surprised either. "Okay, okay," she said. "So I should starve? I'll just make it myself."

The Little Red Hen washed up carefully.

She put a big bowl on the kitchen table. Then she set her timer. According to Jewish law, Passover matzah had to be finished in just eighteen minutes.

The Little Red Hen mixed the flour and water. *Quickly, quickly, quickly.*

She kneaded it. *Quickly, quickly, quickly.*

She rolled it out nice and flat. *Quickly, quickly, quickly.*

She pricked it all over. *Prickly, prickly, prickly.*

She put it into
the oven to bake.

Ding! The matzah was ready, just in time.

Then the Little Red Hen prepared the Seder dinner. She boiled eggs, simmered soup, and mixed gefilte fish. She washed parsley, chopped apples and nuts, and stirred batter for a cake. Finally she set the table, putting a beautiful Passover Haggadah at each place and an extra chair for Elijah the prophet—should he come, God willing. She finished with a covered plate of homemade matzah.

The Little Red Hen sat in a chair and waited. When the sun began to set in the evening sky, there was a knock at the door. Guess who was standing there?

Baa.

Neigh.

Woof.

"We're famished," they told the Little Red Hen. "What's for dinner?"

"You've got to be kidding!" scolded the Little Red Hen. "What chutzpah! You didn't help me plant the grains when I asked you. You didn't help me harvest the wheat, or carry it to the mill, or take it back home again. You didn't even help me bake the matzah. So tell me, why should I share my Seder with the likes of you?"

Sheep, Horse, and Dog couldn't think of a thing to say. The Little Red Hen was right; they hadn't been very good friends. The three animals silently hung their heads in shame.

The Little Red Hen was quiet too. *Now I should invite them to my Seder?* she thought. Then she remembered the words written in the Passover Haggadah: *Let all who are hungry come and eat.* She looked at her friends. They looked hungry. Besides, the Little Red Hen was a good egg—a mensch. A mensch forgives. "And why are you just standing there?" she said finally. "Come on in!"

So together the friends celebrated the holiday. Together they noshed on tasty, crunchy matzah. And when the Seder was over, after all the planting and the harvesting, the schlepping and the cleaning, the baking and the feasting, just who do you think had to wash all those dishes?

"Not I," said the Little Red Hen.

ABOUT PASSOVER

For eight days every spring, Jewish people around the world celebrate the holiday of Passover, the festival of freedom. On the first two nights, family and friends gather for a special holiday dinner called a *Seder*. Before the meal, they read together from Passover books called *Haggadot*. They sing and pray and tell an ancient story.

More than three thousand years ago, the Jewish people were slaves in the land of Egypt, forced to do the bidding of cruel pharaohs. The Jews longed for the day when they would be free. God finally answered their prayers by sending them a man named Moses. "You must go to Pharaoh," God told Moses, "and say, 'Let my people go!'" Moses did so, but Pharaoh would not listen. So God punished the Egyptians with ten plagues, each one worse than the one before. Pharaoh finally agreed to free the Jews. Afraid that he might change his mind, the Jews left immediately, not even waiting for their bread to rise. That is why hard, flat matzah is eaten during Passover—to remember and celebrate the journey from bitter slavery into joyous freedom. Other ceremonial foods are eaten too. At the end of the meal, the door is opened for the prophet Elijah, who, the Jewish people believe, will arrive one day to announce a time of peace for everyone on Earth.

TO MAKE MATZAH

Passover matzah must be made from special Passover flour, using special Passover dishes and utensils—or make it any time of year, just for fun. Ask a grown-up for help with the recipe. See if you can finish in 18 minutes, from the time you pour the water into the flour till the time the matzah comes out of the oven.

1 pound (454 g) flour
¾ cup (177 ml) water, approximately
A large bowl
A kitchen timer
A large spoon
A rolling pin
A fork
A cookie sheet

1. Preheat oven to 500°F (260°C).
2. Pour the flour into a bowl, making a hole in the center. Set the kitchen timer for 18 minutes. Slowly pour the water into the center and use a large spoon to mix in the flour from the sides, little by little.
3. Turn the dough out on a flat floured surface, kneading with your hands until all the flour is incorporated and the dough is no longer sticky. With a rolling pin, roll about half of the dough at a time into a big circle*, nice and thin. Prick it all over with a fork.
4. Bake on an ungreased cookie sheet for 3 to 4 minutes, or until very lightly golden (the thinner the matzah is, the faster it will cook).
5. Cool and dry completely before storing.

*Before there were machines to make the square-shaped matzah most Jews eat today, expert matzah bakers rolled the dough into circles and many other fanciful shapes.

GLOSSARY

The Yiddish language, still spoken by many Jewish people throughout the world, blends mostly Hebrew and German. Some Yiddish words have become part of the English language.

CHUTZPAH: Guts, daring, nerve (usually in a bad sense).

KVETCH: To complain or gripe all the time.

MENSCH: A decent person, someone who is basically good.

NOSH: To eat or snack.

OY GEVALT: An expression of dismay or annoyance, something like "Oh, for Pete's sake!" Alternately, people say "Oy vey" or just "Oy."

SCHLEP: To drag or haul.

PASSOVER FOODS

GEFILTE FISH: Fish patties, traditionally eaten at the Passover Seder, made from ground fish, especially carp.

MATZAH: Flat, crunchy, unleavened bread eaten during Passover.